All Aboard
the Schooltrain

A LITTLE STORY FROM THE GREAT MIGRATION

By Glenda Armand

Illustrated by Keisha Morris

Scholastic Press ◆ New York

"Here comes another one!" I shouted.

It was our last picnic of summer. Pop had borrowed Uncle Al's old truck so we could come watch trains pass by our little country town of Vacherie, Louisiana.

I liked imagining where the passengers were going. And what they would see.

My twin sisters and I jumped and shouted and waved. Passengers waved
back. The engineer tugged his whistle. *Wooh! Woooh!*

"That's the Sunset Limited," Pop announced. "It's going all the way
to California!"

California! Aunt Bea and Uncle Ed had just moved there.
Uncle Ed used to work with Pop at Golden Star Farm.
But a man named Jim Crow had made trouble for
some of the men. Like my best friend
Ann Marie's father, Mr. Foucher.
And Uncle Ed.

So Aunt Bea and Uncle Ed moved away. Aunt Bea wrote
to Mom that California was always sunny and orange trees grew on every
corner. We were sad that they left, but they were happy there. Mom called
it bittersweet when you are happy and sad at the same time. Maybe one
day we would visit them in California. I like oranges!

We watched the Sunset Limited until the caboose disappeared.

"If only I could ride a train!" I wished as we squeezed into the front of the truck for the ride home.

"Thelma," Mom reminded me, "you will be riding a train very soon."

"That's right! A train that has no windows and no wheels," said Pop with a wink. "This train has eyes and feet!"

"What train?" asked Bessie, yawning. The twins were three. Too young to remember.

"The schooltrain!" I answered. "I can't wait to get back on board!"

"Can we ride, too?" asked Betty with droopy eyes.

"Not yet," I said. "Look! The movie tent is back in town!"

"Sure is!" said Pop. "And so is Jim Crow."

On the first day of third grade, I woke up before Peter, our rooster, crowed.
I waved good-bye to Pop as he left for work, carrying his shovel and axe for
digging ditches. I hoped that Mr. Jim Crow wouldn't make any trouble for
him. I didn't want Pop to have to leave like Uncle Ed and Ann Marie's father,
who was all the way up north in Minnesota.

After breakfast, the twins and I sat on the steps, looking and listening.
The schooltrain didn't have a whistle, but we soon heard it coming:

"Schooltrain! Schooltrain! Don't be late!
The school bell rings at half past eight!"

"Get on board, Thelma!" called Ann Marie.

My cousin Chris, a sixth grader, was last in line. "I'm the caboose this year," he bragged.

Mom handed me my lunch pail and I happily got on board behind Ann Marie.

"Watch your step!" Mom called to our engineer, Michael, who was in the eighth grade. "Stay together, children!"

Michael began walking and we followed. Magnolia leaves crunched underfoot. I was back on the schooltrain!

When we turned onto the main road, I waved at Diane. We were only allowed to play together on Saturdays, when Mom worked at Diane's house. And we went to different schools. It would be fun to ride a school bus like she did. But not as much fun as the schooltrain!

We continued on our way, picking up passengers, chanting at every stop:

"Schooltrain! Schooltrain! Don't be late!
The school bell rings at half past eight!"

We passed old folks rocking on their porches.

We passed farmers out in the field.

"Go get that education, children!" they called,

"Old Jim Crow can't take *that* from you!"

Ann Marie's eyes filled with tears. She must have been thinking

of her father. She wrote to him every day. As soon as he found a

job, he said he would send for her and her mom. That meant my

best friend was going to leave me one day. But I did not want

to think about it. Why was Jim Crow so mean?

Our teacher, Miss Clare, was ringing the bell as we arrived at the schoolhouse. With a cheery welcome, she led us inside, where we sat in rows by grade level.

The day began with reading, my favorite subject. Ann Marie cheered up. It was her favorite, too. Each grade rotated to the front row when it was time to read with Miss Clare. She said that reading was the ticket to a good education and a better life.

After lunch, Miss Clare walked between the rows of desks, reading aloud to us. With our imagination and her books, Miss Clare became the engineer, and the potbellied stove, the engine of a magical train.

We traveled back in time to meet great people like Frederick Douglass and Harriet Tubman. They were born into slavery — forced to work for White people for no pay. Frederick and Harriet escaped to freedom, and then they helped free others. How brave they were!

"Slavery ended many years ago," Miss Clare taught us. "But we are still fighting for our rights. We still need courageous people to lead that fight."

And we need courageous people to fight Mr. Jim Crow, I thought.
I wanted to learn to be brave like Harriet Tubman and Frederick
Douglass. "Just keep riding that schooltrain," Pop always said.

So each morning, I was ready when the schooltrain arrived. And rain or shine, it ran on time. One rainy day, Diane was on her bus when we reached the main road.

The other kids on the bus laughed and pointed at us. Not Diane.
She looked sad. It made me and Ann Marie sad, too, to see kids

Michael told us to ignore the mean kids on the bus. So we did. We jumped over puddles and crossed ditches on wobbly boards. Soaked with joy, we raised our voices, singing gleefully:

"Schooltrain! Schooltrain! Don't be late!
The school bell rings at half past eight!"

When we arrived at school, we took off our wet things, dried off by the potbellied stove, and got to work. I wondered where Miss Clare's magic train would take us this afternoon. It had already transported us on great adventures to places like Oz and Lilliput and Treasure Island.

On this wet afternoon, as thunder
roared and lightning cracked, Miss Clare
led us on a thrilling journey from Earth
to the moon! The Sunset Limited
couldn't do that!

In December, the day I did not want to think about came. When the schooltrain arrived at our house, Ann Marie waved a letter over her head. "Daddy found a job!" she shouted with joy. "We'll all be together for Christmas!"

She had the biggest smile on her face that I had ever seen. I tried to smile, too, but I missed her already.

On Ann Marie's last day of school, she told us all about Minnesota. "The same Mississippi River that runs through Vacherie begins in Minnesota!"

She was so happy. That was the sweet part.

That afternoon, when the schooltrain dropped me off, Ann Marie and I hugged and cried. We were both losing our best friend. This was the the bitter part. We promised to write every day.

Before long, Christmas vacation was over. When I boarded the schooltrain for the first time in the new year, I carried three letters from Ann Marie in my coat pocket. All day, whenever I felt sad, I read one. I still had Diane, but I could only see her once a week.

Dear Thelma,

How are you? Fine, I hope. We got here safely. We only spent one night on the train. We were happy to see Daddy. And he was happy to see us. It is so cold! They say we are going to have a white Christmas. That means it's going to snow. I miss you. Tell your mom and pop and the twins I said hello.

Your best friend,

Ann Marie

Dear Thelma,

I got your letter. I h   eling better. Did you hav   ?
Some ki   our a
                      build a
                      eps to g
apart   hat the
apartments
hello to your mom an
Still your best friend

Ann Marie

When I walked to the corner to meet Pop after school, I asked him a question I had been thinking about for a long time. "Pop, why can't Diane ride the schooltrain with us to our school? Those kids on her school bus are mean."

Pop smiled but his eyes looked sad. "Because of Jim Crow, Thelma."

"Pop, who is Jim Crow?" I asked. "Why does he like to make people unhappy?"

"Jim Crow is not a person, Thelma," Pop said.

"Not a person? Then who . . . what?" I didn't know what to ask!

"Jim Crow," Pop said, "is a name for the unfair laws and rules here in the South that treat White people better than Black people. Diane's school has new books and desks."

"Our books fall apart and our desks are wobbly. That's not fair," I said. "Pop, is Jim Crow the reason we can't go to the movies with Diane's family?"

"Yep. Jim Crow laws are meant to keep Black and White people apart."

When the last day of school arrived, Michael received his eighth grade diploma. His family was moving to New Orleans, where he could go to high school. "I want to be a real engineer," he told us, "and there's no high school for us in Vacherie. Because of Jim Crow!"

I raised my hand. "Miss Clare, maybe Jim Crow isn't a real person, but the laws hurt real people!"

Miss Clare nodded. "But remember, boys and girls, with education and courage, you can do away with Jim Crow."

I promised myself I would remember.

Two weeks later, I was sitting on the porch writing a letter to Ann Marie when Pop showed up early. He tossed his tools into the toolshed without cleaning and sharpening them. Pop never did that. He didn't even say hello. Uh-oh. Something was wrong. My hand shook and my heart pounded as Pop went inside.

At supper, right after we said grace, I blurted out, "Pop, did you break a
Jim Crow law?"

"Yes," Mom answered proudly. "He spoke up when his boss did something
wrong."

"That was brave, Pop!" I exclaimed. But then I remembered something.
And my heart pounded again. "Pop, will you be punished?"

He looked at me and the twins. "I was fired."

"Things need to change," Pop said, "but we can't wait."

"We're moving to Los Angeles," Mom said. "We'll stay with Uncle Ed and Aunt Bea."

"We are?" I exclaimed. "We're going to ride on a real train?"

"Yay!" Bessie and Betty clapped and cheered.

I did not know what to think. "This is bittersweet," I said.

Mom and Pop smiled. "The important thing," said Mom, "is that we will all be together."

Right away, we started preparing to leave. I finished my letter to
Ann Marie and gave her our new address. Boy, would she be surprised!
As I helped Mom pack, I wondered what Los Angeles would be like.
It had plenty of oranges and sunshine, but would I make friends there?

The five of us went to the home of every neighbor, relative, and
friend to say good-bye. Finally, it was time to leave for the train station
in New Orleans.

At the station, we hugged and kissed everyone who had come to see us off. I would miss them all. I planned to write to Diane and Chris. Mom tearfully declared that no matter where we lived, Vacherie would always be home.

I thanked Miss Clare for the adventures on the potbellied train. I told her I was worried about going to a new school. She hugged me and gave me a book. "You'll be just fine," she promised. "You have your ticket."

We boarded the Sunset Limited. As the train chugged out of the station, the twins and I pressed against the window. We waved at well-wishers. They waved back.

After a while, Bessie and Betty fell asleep. Mom and Pop whispered
plans for our new life. As I watched fields of sugarcane zoom by, I was back
on another train — the one with eyes and feet. I could see us dodging mother
hens, feeling the rain as we jumped over puddles. I could taste the blackberries
and smell the magnolia blossoms. I could even hear the old folks
saying: "Go get that education, children!" I smiled and chanted softly:

"Schooltrain! Schooltrain! Don't be late!
The school bell rings at half past eight!"

Yes, I would always remember the schooltrain. But today, at last,
I was aboard the Sunset Limited, off on a great adventure. And I
planned to enjoy the ride — all the way to California.

A Note from the Author

THERE REALLY WAS A SCHOOLTRAIN. *All Aboard the Schooltrain* is inspired by one of my mother's childhood memories. Mom grew up in the tiny, rural town of Vacherie, fifty miles west of New Orleans, Louisiana, in the 1920s and '30s. She had fond memories of walking to school single file with friends and relatives, singing all the way. She was the second oldest of eight children. The youngest were her twin sisters, Bessie and Betty. To tell the story, I used elements of my mother's life and of my own childhood.

Unlike the main character, the real Thelma left Louisiana when she was an adult. She and my dad, Augustus, grew up there — Mom in "Back" (South) Vacherie and Dad in "Front" (North) Vacherie. Both families' roots in Vacherie go back to the early 1700s. Creole was Mom's first language, and she never lost her accent. While Mom rode the schooltrain to a little red schoolhouse, Dad went to "private school," as he liked to say. His neighbor taught children in her kitchen. Tuition was a nickel a week.

Mom and Dad married right after Dad came back from fighting in World War II. They moved to New Orleans and had four children, including me, the youngest. When my parents decided, in the early 1950s, to move to Los Angeles, they did not know we were participating in a history-changing event called the Great Migration.

Between 1915 and 1970, around six million African Americans left the South and, traveling by car, bus, and train, headed west, north, and northeast. They left to find work and to escape the brutal Jim Crow laws that made life difficult and often dangerous for Black people. The term "Jim Crow" dates back to the early 1830s. A White actor painted his face black and performed a show in which he played a clumsy, slow character he called "Jim Crow." As the show's popularity spread, "Jim Crow" became a derogatory term for Black people. Although Jim Crow's popularity as a fictional character eventually died out, "Jim Crow" became a term for describing anti-Black laws.

Many Black people lost their lives due to Jim Crow laws. In Vacherie, the lack of opportunities for Black people was the main form of Jim Crow racism. While there were instances of racial violence, White and Black people, for the most part, obeyed Jim Crow rules that were unwritten and rarely disputed: They went to separate schools and different churches (or sat on opposite sides of the aisle), and did not intermarry. Signs such as WHITES ONLY and COLORED ENTRANCE were found in big cities like New Orleans, not in "the country," where everyone, White and Black, knew one another. Signs like THURSDAY IS COLORED NIGHT would be unnecessary. Everyone would have known. I felt it important for readers to see the sign as a way to illustrate those unspoken rules. "Colored" was an acceptable term at the time this story takes place. Today, the term "Colored" to identify people is outdated and disrespectful.

In the story, Thelma's family migrates in the 1930s, during the first wave of the Great Migration, 1915–1940. During that time, many well-known people in all fields of endeavor blossomed in Great Migration destination cities. These migrants included the parents of Toni Morrison, who left Alabama and Georgia and settled in Ohio, where the Pulitzer Prize–winning writer was born. Rock & Roll Hall of Fame singer Aretha Franklin moved from Tennessee to New York City and, later, Detroit, Michigan. Michelle Obama's ancestors migrated from South Carolina and Georgia to Chicago, Illinois, where the former First Lady was born.

Unlike the family in the story, my family joined the second wave of the Great Migration, 1945–1970. We took the Southern Pacific Railroad's Sunset Limited to California and stayed with my dad's brother and sister-in-law, Uncle Ed and Aunt Bea, until we found a place of our own. My three younger siblings were born in Los Angeles.

Notable migrants of the second wave of the Great Migration include award-winning film producer Spike Lee, who moved from Georgia to New York, and Condoleezza Rice, the first Black female US secretary of state, who migrated with her parents from Alabama to Colorado.

Throughout the history of Africans in America, there has been a train: a way to freedom, a chance for a better life. The train took many forms: the Underground Railroad, a brave leader, a steel locomotive, or a '57 Ford station wagon. Sometimes it was the simple ability to read and write. Frederick Douglass said, "Once you learn to read, you will be forever free."

All Aboard the Schooltrain represents the three trains that my family "rode" to freedom: the Sunset Limited, getting that education, and a love of books. Signing up for a public library card was a cherished rite of passage for us. My parents, whose formal education ended with the eighth grade, were great believers in the importance of education. Dad was a wonderful writer. Both were great storytellers.

When he was stationed in the Philippines during the war, Dad wrote over two hundred letters to Mom, complete with metaphors and similes that make the English teacher in me proud. Mom always prefaced her stories with, "I'm not going to tell this right," and then proceeded to weave a tale complete with rising action, climax, falling action, and denouement. Both were lifelong gardeners: Dad, vegetables; Mom, flowers. But, after God and family, education was all-important. Thus, my parents saw to it that all seven of their children received college degrees.

The Great Migration produced profound changes in the people and places involved. The decision to stay or go was an agonizing one. As a child of the Great Migration, I have deep respect for those who chose to leave in search of a better life, as well as for those who decided to stay and work to bring about change and make life better in the places they called *home*.

Thelma's Family Photographs

The Vacherie family home where Thelma and her seven siblings grew up, built c. 1915.

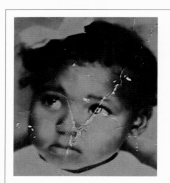 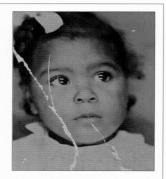

Thelma's twin sisters, Bessie and Betty, about 1 year old.

Thelma, posing for a traveling photographer, Vacherie, c. 1940.

Gus in his military uniform, MacDill Airfield, Tampa, Florida, 1941.

The author's parents Thelma Jones Armand and Augustus (Gus) Armand on their wedding day in Vacherie, 1946.

Thelma, Gus, and children. Back row, born in Louisiana: Glenda (the author), Jenny, Troy, Nelda. Front row, born in Los Angeles: Chris, Valerie, Faynessa, 1962.

Though Thelma and Gus didn't have the opportunity to be educated beyond the eighth grade, they put all their children through college. Back row: Faynessa, Pitzer College (sociology/Black studies); Glenda, Pomona College (English literature); Jenny, California State University, Dominguez Hills (sociology); Valerie, University of Southern California (geology); Chris, Cal State Dominguez Hills (business economics/accounting). Front row: Nelda, California State University, Long Beach (history); Troy, Cal State Long Beach (electrical engineering).

Aunt Bea and Uncle Ed at a family gathering in Los Angeles, c. 1970.

The author's grandmother (Noemie), mother (Thelma), Glenda, and daughter (Leah) at their family home in Los Angeles, 1988.

Thelma and Gus Armand and four of their five daughters, posing for a newspaper article in the backyard of the family home in Los Angeles. From left, Faynessa, Jenny, Nelda, and Glenda, 1994.

Gus 92, and Thelma 91, at home in Los Angeles.

Sources

- Anderson, James D. *The Education of Blacks in the South, 1860–1935*. Chapel Hill: The University of North Carolina Press, 1988.
- Armand, Faynessa (sister). "Unwritten Rules." Interviewed June–October 2020.
- Armand, Thelma (mother). "We Rode the Schooltrain." Interviewed February 2013.
- Hofsommer, Don L. *The Southern Pacific, 1901–1985*. College Station: Texas A&M University Press, 1986.
- Pablo, Obie (family friend, born in 1933). "Vacherie Was Paradise." Interviewed June 2020.
- Steib, Joseph (Al), (cousin). "The Tracks Ran along the River." Interviewed September 2020.
- Wilkerson, Isabel. *The Warmth of Other Suns: The Epic Story of America's Great Migration*. New York: Random House, 2010.

Literature Referenced

- Baum, L. Frank. *The Wonderful Wizard of Oz*. Chicago: George M. Hill Company, 1900.
- Stevenson, Robert Louis. *Treasure Island*. London: Cassell and Company, 1883.
- Swift, Jonathan. *Gulliver's Travels*. Ireland: Benjamin Motte, 1726.
- Verne, Jules. *From the Earth to the Moon*. Translated by Thomas H. Linklater. London: Ward Lock & Co., 1877.

Photos

Photos ©: 38 top: Courtesy of Glenda Armand, Vacherie family home; 38 middle: Courtesy of Amber Ned, Thelma's twin sisters; Courtesy of Glenda Armand, wedding day; 38 bottom: Courtesy of Glenda Armand, Thelma; Courtesy of Glenda Armand, Gus; 39 top: Courtesy of Glenda Armand, Thelma, Gus, and children; Courtesy of Glenda Armand, Armand children; 39 middle: Courtesy of Diana Armand, Aunt Bea and Uncle Ed; Courtesy of Glenda Armand, four generations of Armand women; 39 bottom: Courtesy of Glenda Armand, newspaper article; Courtesy of Glenda Armand, Gus and Thelma.

In memory of my mother,

who saved her best story for last. — GA

For Jocelyn and Jocelyn. — KM

Text copyright © 2023 by Glenda Armand ◆ Artwork copyright © 2023 by Keisha Morris ◆ All rights reserved. Published by Scholastic Press, an imprint of Scholastic Inc., *Publishers since 1920*. SCHOLASTIC, SCHOLASTIC PRESS, and associated logos are trademarks and/or registered trademarks of Scholastic Inc. ◆ The publisher does not have any control over and does not assume any responsibility for author or third-party websites or their content. ◆ No part of this publication may be reproduced, stored in a retrieval system, or transmitted in any form or by any means, electronic, mechanical, photocopying, recording, or otherwise, without written permission of the publisher. For information regarding permission, write to Scholastic Inc., Attention: Permissions Department, 557 Broadway, New York, NY 10012.

LIBRARY OF CONGRESS CATALOGING-IN-PUBLICATION DATA AVAILABLE
ISBN 978-1-338-76689-9 ◆ 10 9 8 7 6 5 4 3 2 1   23 24 25 26 27 ◆ Printed in China 62 ◆ First edition, January 2023

Keisha Morris's art was created with layered tissue paper that was collaged together using Photoshop ◆ The display type was set in Central Station Std Bold ◆ The text type was set in Baskerville TT Regular ◆ The book was printed and bound at Leo Paper. ◆ Production was overseen by Jaime Chan. ◆ Manufacturing was supervised by Irene Chan. ◆ The book was art directed and designed by Marijka Kostiw, and edited by Tracy Mack.